MW00899928

This book is dedicated to all my past and present blind dogs--- Lupe, Tootsie, Stanley, Porkchop, Chester, Grover and Woody --- all of whom have refused to allow their blindness to stand in the way of happiness, joy and love.

BLIND DOGS CAN'T FETCH

BUT BLIND DOGS
LOVE TO PLAY
TUG OF WAR

BLIND DOGS CAN'T CHASE RABBITS FROM THE GARDEN

BUT BLIND DOGS CAN HELP YOU WITH THE PLANTING

BLIND DOGS CAN'T GO HIKING WITH YOU

BUT BLIND DOGS LOVE GOING WITH YOU ON ROAD TRIPS

BLIND DOGS CAN'T BRING IN THE NEWSPAPER

BUT BLIND DOGS
CAN WARM
YOUR FEET
WHILE YOU
READ IT

BLIND DOGS CAN'T ALERT YOU THAT THE MAIL IS ARRIVING

BUT BLIND DOGS CAN CHEER YOU UP WHEN YOU READ THE BILLS

BLIND DOGS CAN'T GO JOGGING WITH YOU

BUT BLIND DOGS CAN INSPIRE YOU DURING YOUR WORKOUTS

BLIND DOGS CAN'T HERD SHEEP

BUT BLIND DOGS CAN HELP YOU COUNT THEM

BLIND DOGS CAN'T BE SEEING EYE GUIDES

BUT BLIND DOGS CAN BE GREAT THERAPY DOGS

BLIND DOGS CAN'T LOOK YOU IN THE EYES

BUT BLIND DOGS CAN GIVE YOU LOTS OF KISSES

BLIND DOGS CAN'T DO EVERYTHING SIGHTED DOGS CAN DO

BUT BLIND DOGS CAN STILL LOVE YOU WITH ALL THEIR HEARTS

THE END

CPSIA information can be obtained
at www.ICGtesting.com
Printed in the USA
FSOW03n2304250716
22933FS